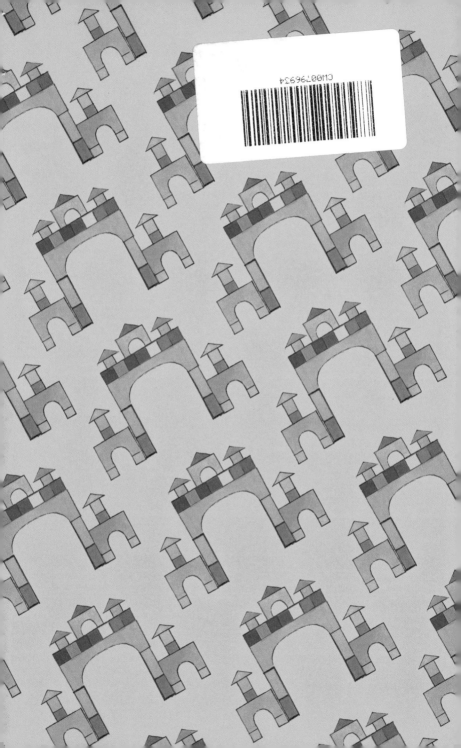

THIS

Enid Blyton

BOOK BELONGS TO

NODDY

HURRAH FOR LITTLE NODDY

There are ten classic Noddy stories for you to enjoy ...

Noddy Goes to Toyland

Hurrah for Little Noddy

Noddy and his Car

Here Comes Noddy

Well Done, Noddy

Noddy Goes to School

Noddy at the Seaside

Noddy and the Magic Rubber

Noddy and Tessie Bear

Noddy Gets into Trouble

Enid Blyton

NODDY

HURRAH FOR LITTLE NODDY

Hodder
Children's
Books

HODDER CHILDREN'S BOOKS

First published in Great Britain in 1949 by Samson Low
This edition published in 2016 by Hodder and Stoughton

2 4 6 8 10 9 7 5 3 1

A CIP catalogue record for this book
is available from the British Library.

ISBN 978-1-444-93293-5

Printed in China

The paper and board used in this book are from wood from responsible sources.

Hodder Children's Books
An imprint of
Hachette Children's Group
Part of Hodder and Stoughton
Carmelite House
50 Victoria Embankment
London EC4Y 0DZ

An Hachette UK Company
www.hachette.co.uk

www.hachettechildrens.co.uk

'Milko! Milko!' shouted a voice just outside Tubby Cottage. Mr Tubby the teddy bear lived there, and his wife put her head out of the window.

'Two bottles, please,' she called. 'And oh, milkman, you'd better call at the house next door – the little new one, called House-for-One. Mr Noddy lives there, and he may want some milk.'

'That house wasn't there yesterday when I came round with the milk,' said the little wooden milkman in surprise.

'No, it wasn't. Mr Noddy only came yesterday,' said Mrs Tubby. 'He and Big-Ears the brownie built it with toy bricks. It's nice, isn't it?'

'Milko! Milko!' he called just outside Noddy's window. The little nodding man was asleep, but he woke up with a jump and went to the door, his head nid-nodding madly.

'Good morning,' he said. 'Yes, I would like some milk.'

'One bottle? Two bottles?' asked the wooden milkman. Noddy nodded hard.

'Well, say which you want,' said the milkman. 'You nod for one bottle, and you nod for two! How am I to know which you want?'

'Oh, don't take any notice of my nodding head,' said Noddy. 'I'm made like that. Look, my head is fixed on my neck on a kind of spring – and if you tap me, I nod very hard indeed!'

'Do let me tap you then,' said the milkman, and he tapped Noddy's head smartly. At once his head began to nod up and down very fast. The milkman laughed and laughed.

He gave Noddy a bottle of milk.

'One penny, please,' he said.

'Oh goodness – I forgot. I haven't any money,' said Noddy, in dismay.

'Well, you can pay me by letting me tap your head each morning until you've got some money,' said the milkman, with a grin. 'I'd like that!'

Noddy went indoors with his milk. He had no furniture at all except for a chair that Mr Tubby had lent him to sleep in. Dear, dear – he really must get a job and earn some money! Mrs Tubby arrived with a boiled egg and some bread and butter on a plate.

'You're a very kind teddy indeed,' said Noddy. 'I do wish I knew how to get some work to do. Do you know anyone who wants a very willing workman, Mrs Tubby?'

'Well, you might go and try at Four-Chimney House,' said Mrs Tubby. 'They're spring cleaning, you know. It's quite a big doll's house. If you can scrub and polish I should think they'd pay you well.'

'I'll go this very morning,' said Noddy, happily. 'Isn't the house I built lovely, Mrs Tubby? I do feel proud of it.'

The little nodding man put on his pointed hat with the jingling bell at the top. He rubbed his shoes with a bit of paper, because he hadn't even a shoe-brush. Then he set off to find Four-Chimney House.

It was quite easy to find because it was the only house with four chimneys. It was a very nice doll's house, with a garage at the side, and a flower garden at the front. A little blue car was in the garage.

Noddy went round to the back door. A small doll in a big white apron opened the door.

She had curly golden hair and bright blue
eyes. She looked at Noddy, and he bowed,
his head nodding all the time.

'What do you want?' she said. 'Are you the
laundry man, or the chimney-sweep?'

'No, I'm only Noddy,' said Noddy. 'I heard
you were spring cleaning. I'm sure I would be
good at that, because I've got plenty of spring in
me, and I'm full of leaps and bounds.'

'That's nothing to do with spring cleaning,' said the little doll. 'We're cleaning the house because it's springtime, silly. Come in. I'll see if I can find something for you to do.'

The little doll thought for a moment. 'The sweep hasn't come,' she said. 'I suppose you don't know how to sweep chimneys, do you?'

'I'm sure I could sweep your four chimneys,' said Noddy, at once. 'I'll try.'

So he was set to work to sweep the chimneys.

He poked the brush up each chimney, and the little doll-children ran outside so that they could tell him when the brush came out at the top.

'You've done very well,' said the golden-haired doll, when he had swept all the chimneys.

Next Noddy set to work to scrub the big kitchen floor. He did it so well that everyone came to see how nice it was.

'You're a very good worker,' said the doll. 'Now will you please carry some rubbish out to

the bottom of the back garden for me, and put it
on the bonfire to burn?'

Well, he was given all sorts of things to take
down to the bonfire. He was given an old bed, a
broken chair, a table whose top was cracked, and
a carpet with holes in it. Noddy didn't put them
on the bonfire. He stood and looked at them all
lying in a heap where he had tipped them out of
his barrow.

'Why, I could mend that bed and sleep on it,' he thought. 'And that chair would just fit me. And that table would look so nice in my little house if I mended it and painted it! And that carpet just wants patching and it would be so bright and cosy on my floor!'

He ran to ask the golden-haired doll if he could have the things for himself instead of burning them.

'Would you really like all that old stuff?' said the golden-haired doll, in surprise.

Noddy nodded like anything. 'Oh yes, yes! It would be just right for me.'

So that night Noddy piled heaps and heaps of old things on his barrow, and wheeled them to House-for-One. He called out to fat Mr Tubby as he passed.

'A bed to sleep in, a chair to sit on, a table to eat off, a carpet to walk on! A plate and a cup and a dish! An old knife and fork and spoon! A little cracked wash basin! I'm the happiest fellow in the world, Mr Tubby!'

Noddy spent a happy evening mending all the things he had been given. You should have seen how different his little house looked with a bit of furniture in it!

He had been paid some money for his work that day. He bought his supper and his breakfast out of it, and the rest he put away to give Big-Ears.

'He lent me such a lot of money,' thought Noddy, nodding his head as he remembered. 'People must always pay back what they borrow. I will put some of my pennies into the drawer of the table. Then I can give them to Big-Ears when he comes.'

For three more days Noddy worked hard at Four-Chimney House. The golden-haired doll gave him such a lot of things she didn't want. She even gave him old curtains, and how nice his windows looked when he put them up. They were red curtains, with stripes, and they looked very cheerful indeed.

More money went into the kitchen drawer. Noddy began to feel quite rich.

But after the three days were up the golden-haired doll didn't want him to work any more.

'Our spring cleaning is finished,' she said. 'Why don't you go to the Toy Garage and ask if you can help to clean the cars there?'

The garage had a toy petrol station, and was really rather grand. Tiny cars drove up for petrol. Others came in for cleaning and polishing. The owner of the garage was a kindly-looking doll called Mr Sparks.

'Yes, you can come and clean cars for me,' he said. 'My man is away. You can have his job until he comes back.'

Noddy set to work happily. He liked the bright little cars. They were all colours: red, blue, yellow, green and orange.

'Oh, if only I had a car of my own!' thought Noddy. 'Wouldn't that be lovely? But I shall never, never be rich enough to own one.'

He pressed the horn, and it hooted: 'Parp, parp, parp!'

Mr Sparks, the garage owner, almost jumped out of his skin. 'Hey!' he shouted. 'You're supposed to clean the cars, not toot the horns! You get on with your work!'

'Sorry,' said Noddy, and he set to work to clean and polish. Soon he could see his face in the bonnet of every single car. Mr Sparks was very pleased.

'Come tomorrow,' he said. 'And here's your pay. You're a good worker.'

'More money!' thought Noddy, pleased, as he hurried home that night. 'Half to put away for Big-Ears, and half to spend on myself.'

For a whole week Noddy worked at the Toy Garage. Then the other man came back and Mr Sparks said he wouldn't need him any more. Noddy was very sad.

'Oh dear – now I've got to get another job,' he thought. 'I must get one quickly, too, or my money will all go.'

He went home thinking so hard about it that he left his little hat behind, the one with the bell on top.

'Bother!' he said. 'I've forgotten my hat. I'll go and fetch it after I've had my supper!'

After he had had his supper that night, Noddy set off to fetch his cap from the garage.

He came to the garage just as the moon sailed

out of the clouds – and he saw something that puzzled him very much!

'The garage door is open!' said Noddy, surprised. 'Who is there at this time of night?'

Then he heard a noise. 'R-r-r-r-r-r! R-r-r-r-r-r!'

'Well! Someone is going to run a car out of the garage!' thought Noddy. 'In the middle of the night! Can it be a thief – someone who has come to steal one of Mr Sparks' cars?'

He stood in the shadows and watched. Out came a car, driven by a little goblin. Then another – and another – and another!

Noddy was so surprised that he couldn't even shout. Why – it wasn't just one car that was being stolen – it was all of them!

Noddy suddenly knew he must do something about this. But what could he do? There were so many goblins – one to each car – and all the cars were racing out of the garage as fast as they could go!

Noddy remembered a little old car that stood in a shed nearby. He ran to see if it was there. Yes, it was.

'I'll get in it and drive after the thieves!' thought Noddy, bravely. 'I can't fight them, there are too many – but at least I can follow them and see where they go.'

He got into the funny little car. He started it. It ran noisily out of the old shed and down the pathway to the road. Off he went. He had never driven a car before, but he didn't mind. He knew how to steer, and although he wobbled a bit, he kept the car on the road.

All through Toyland he went, and out into the country. Far away ahead all the other cars raced at sixty miles an hour. Noddy followed, turning corners on two wheels, and yelling at any rabbit that was in his way.

He went quite a long way – and then something dreadful happened!

A wheel came off his car! It was such a very old car, and one of the front wheels had always been loose. It rolled down the road, scared a peeping rabbit, and ran into a bush. The car spun round on its three wheels, and crashed into a tree.

Noddy flew right up in the air out of the car, the steering wheel still in his hands. He landed in the middle of a bush, which was very lucky for him.

A small, frightened voice called out to him: 'What's happened? Who are you out there?'

Noddy knew that voice. It was the voice of Big-Ears the brownie, his very best friend! Oh, what a bit of luck!

'Big-Ears!' called Noddy. 'Oh Big-Ears! It's me. Noddy, you know. I've had an accident.'

Big-Ears the brownie came out into the moonlight, looking scared.

'Noddy! I can't believe it. Were you driving a car? In the middle of the night, too. You must be crazy.'

'No, I'm not crazy. I was chasing thieves,' said Noddy, standing up.

'Well Noddy, it's nice to see you. Come to my toadstool house. You can sleep there tonight,' said Big-Ears.

Big-Ears' house was a large toadstool, with a door in the thick stalk, and a tiny stairway going up to the head of the toadstool.

'This is nice,' said Noddy, his head nodding merrily once more. 'Big-Ears, a whole lot of goblins went to Mr Sparks' garage tonight and took every one of the cars there. I followed them as far as here.'

'Oh I know where they are,' said Big-Ears at once. 'They've gone to the Goblin Village, I'm sure. Goblins love cars, you know, but they always drive so fast that the police won't let them have any.'

'Well, I never! Then I can go back to Mr Sparks' garage tomorrow and tell him where to look for the cars!' said Noddy, delighted. 'Won't he be so very pleased?'

'Very,' said Big-Ears. 'We'll go peeping into Goblin Village tomorrow to see what we can find!'

Noddy was very surprised in the morning to find himself in Big-Ears' toadstool house. But he soon remembered everything that had happened.

'You'd better not go to Goblin Village,' Big-Ears said to Noddy. 'They would wonder why someone from Toyland was there. I'll go and peep round. They know me quite well.'

At the Goblin Village, all the goblins were very excited indeed. They took no notice of Big-Ears.

'My car's blue,' said one.

'Mine's yellow,' said another. 'Oooh, won't we have fun at nights, racing around the woods!'

'Where are the cars?' asked a goblin boy.

'Well, you can just peep at them,' said a goblin. 'They're down that rabbit-hole by the oak tree, all neatly garaged in a row!'

Well, well – that was all that Big-Ears wanted to know! He shot off at once back to his toadstool house to get Noddy.

Big-Ears could pedal very fast indeed on his bicycle. His feet went up and down like lightning. He rang his bell loudly all the way. Everyone skipped out of his path.

As they got near Toy Town Noddy felt rather afraid.

'Big-Ears,' he said, 'I feel scared.'

'Why?' asked the brownie in surprise.

'Well – I took that car and smashed it up, you know,' said Noddy. 'What do you suppose Mr Sparks will say to that? I shouldn't have taken the car, should I? And I certainly shouldn't have smashed it up! Oh dear me!'

'Never mind. They'll get back all their cars because of you,' said Big-Ears. 'I think you were very brave, Noddy.'

They rode into Toy Town. What a to-do there

was there! Mr Sparks was in a terrible state. All his cars were gone! Yes, even the old one out of the shed!

Jumbo was there, waving his trunk about, very upset that his grand car had been stolen. The three Skittles were looking very angry. The Wobbly Man was wobbling to and fro more than ever, he was so worried.

There were crowds of excited toys all about the market place, talking about the stolen cars. Mr Plod, the big toy policeman was there, taking notes from Mr Sparks. Mr Sparks held up Noddy's little pointed hat with its jingling bell.

'I found this,' he said in a loud voice. 'And we all know who this belongs to! It's Noddy's – the little nodding man's! What was his hat doing in the garage last night?'

'He stole the cars!' cried everyone. 'And he dropped his hat by mistake. We must find Noddy.'

Big-Ears jumped off his bicycle nearby at that very moment, and the crowd saw Noddy behind him.

'There he is! There he is!' they cried. 'Catch him, Mr Plod. Put him in prison!'

And before poor Noddy knew what was happening the policeman had caught hold of him, and with Mr Sparks on the other side, he was marched off to prison!

'He stole the cars!' cried everyone. 'What a rogue he is!'

Poor Noddy, he struggled and shouted but it wasn't a bit of good, Mr Sparks and the policeman wouldn't let him go. He looked round for Big-Ears, but the little brownie was quite lost in the crowd.

'I didn't steal the cars, I didn't, I didn't!' cried Noddy. 'I came to tell you where they are.'

'Ho! You did, did you? Well, of course you know where they are, if you stole them,' said Mr Sparks.

And before poor Noddy could say another word he was shut up in the police station in a horrid little cell with only one barred window very high up! How sad he was!

At that moment he heard a tremendous hammering at the door of the police station. Bang, bang, bang, blim-blam, BANG! Then he heard a voice.

'Let me in! I've got something to say. LET ME IN! I'm Big-Ears the brownie, and I want to tell you all about Noddy, and how brave he's been.'

'What's all this?' said Mr Plod, sternly.

'You listen to me, Mr Plod,' said Big-Ears, fiercely. 'Last night Noddy went back to find his cap because he'd left it in the garage.'

'Don't believe it,' said Mr Sparks, who was there.

'And he found the garage door open, and there were goblins inside – and they drove your cars out one by one, Mr Sparks. And Noddy was very brave, he got that old car out of the nearby shed, and drove it full-tilt after them!'

'Good gracious!' said Mr Sparks. 'Is this true? Did he really?'

'Yes, he did,' went on Big-Ears. 'And what's more, we know where the cars are hidden!'

'Where? Tell me where!' cried Mr Sparks; and the policeman looked most excited.

'I shan't tell you,' said Big-Ears. 'You've been horrid and unkind to my friend Mr Noddy. You've locked him up – that good, kind, brave Noddy.'

'Tell us where the cars are, please, please do!' begged Mr Sparks. 'We'll set Mr Noddy free, of course we will!'

'Well I think Noddy deserves a reward, not a punishment, for the brave thing he did,' said Big-Ears. 'I shall tell him not to say a word about where all the cars are unless you give him a fine reward.'

'Well, I must say I think he deserves a reward,' said the policeman. 'What do you think he would like?'

'Well,' said Big-Ears, taking a big breath.
'Well – I think that as he saved everyone else's
cars he ought at least to have a little car of his
own – even if it's a very, very little tiny one!'

Mr Sparks looked at the policeman, and the
policeman looked back at Mr Sparks.

'We shouldn't really have locked him up
without hearing what he had to say,' said the
policeman.

'He must have been very brave to chase those
tiresome goblins,' said Mr Sparks. He turned to
Big-Ears.

'Very well. I will give Noddy a little tiny car of
his own, in return for what he did. But now you must
tell me where the goblins have hidden the cars.'

'Ask Noddy,' said Big-Ears. So to Noddy's
great surprise, his cell door was opened, and he
was taken out very kindly by the policeman and
given a big cup of hot coffee and an enormous
slice of ginger cake.

'We beg your pardon for locking you up,' said Mr Plod, rather red in the face.

'We want to reward you for your bravery,' said Mr Sparks. 'Please tell us where the stolen cars are, brave Mr Noddy.'

'Well – the goblins hid them down the rabbit hole by the old oak tree in Goblin Village,' said Noddy, his head beginning to nod again. 'I'll take you there. I don't really want any reward, though. I'm dreadfully sorry for breaking up your old car, Mr Sparks.'

'Ah – wait and see what your reward is to be before you say you don't want it!' said Mr Sparks, with a smile.

Lots of exciting things happened after that. Mr Plod called six other policemen, and they all got into a big bus with Mr Sparks, Big-Ears, the three Skittles, Jumbo the elephant, Mr Wobbly, the Sailor Doll, three other toys whose cars had been stolen – and Noddy, of course.

He was next to Jumbo, who squashed him dreadfully, but Noddy was so pleased at suddenly being a hero that he really didn't mind. He had his hat back again, too, and it was nice to hear its little bell jingling as his head nodded up and down.

They arrived in Goblin Village. Gobbo, the chief goblin, was called out to see the policemen. He was most alarmed.

'Take me to where you have hidden the stolen cars,' commanded Mr Plod.

'We haven't stolen any,' said Gobbo, sulkily.

'Then take me to the rabbit hole by the old oak tree,' ordered Mr Plod. All the listening goblins howled in fear then, and ran away at top speed.

Gobbo was a bit braver than the rest. He went with them to the rabbit hole – and there were all the cars!

'Just look – all parked nose to tail in a neat row!' said Mr Sparks, amazed. 'Gobbo, who stole them?'

But Gobbo wouldn't tell.

'Very well – I shall fine every single person in Goblin Village one large round penny,' said Mr Plod, firmly. 'That will teach them not to go stealing toy cars again!'

And everyone had to line up and put one large brown penny into one of the policemen's helmets. It was very heavy when the last goblin had thrown his penny in!

Then Jumbo got into his car, the three Skittles got into theirs, and the Sailor Doll got into his.

Mr Sparks got into his own best car, Mr Wobbly wobbled his way to his – and soon all the cars had their right owners at the steering-wheels.

The policemen, Big-Ears and Noddy went home in the bus. Mr Plod let Noddy drive the bus for a treat, and he was too excited for words.

He drove very carefully indeed, and felt very happy. 'I do like driving,' he told Big-Ears. 'It's a lovely feeling. I do wish I had a car of my own – my very own! But I shall never be rich enough to buy one, shall I, Big-Ears?'

'Never!' said Big-Ears, and smiled a little secret smile all to himself. 'What a pity, Noddy, what a pity.'

They all got back to Toy Town at last – and dear me, whilst they had gone, the news had gone round the town about Noddy's cleverness in chasing the goblins and finding out where the stolen cars were.

So what do you think? There was a big feast prepared in the market place for Noddy, Big-Ears and all their friends! My goodness, you should have seen the jellies shivering in their dishes, the plates of sandwiches, the great big chocolate cakes, the buns and biscuits. It really was a wonderful sight!

'Is this for us?' said Noddy in surprise. 'Oh my – is this the reward Mr Sparks said I could have? It's lovely!'

'No, no – that isn't the reward you're going to have,' said Mr Sparks, gruffly. 'Look – there's your reward over there – sitting by itself in the middle of the market place, Noddy!'

Noddy looked. He saw a car – a very little car, just big enough for two people. It was red and yellow. And it had an enormous blue bow tied to the steering-wheel with a message written on a piece of paper.

'To Noddy. He got back our cars – so now he shall have one for himself!'

Noddy's head nodded so wildly that his bell jingled all the time. He couldn't believe his eyes.

'Is it for me? Really for me?' he kept saying. 'Oh, I can't believe it! It can't be mine!'

'Well, you come and join the feast – and afterwards you can drive your new car round and round the market place!' said Mr Sparks. 'But we'll have the feast first – just in case you run into something and take your appetite away!'

So they all sat down to the feast, and it wasn't long before all the dishes were empty. Mr Tubby the teddy bear called out for three cheers for Mr Noddy, and goodness me, what a noise there was!

And then came the happiest moment of Noddy's day. He got into his own little car! He pressed the hooter. 'Parp-parp,' it said proudly.

'There's room for a friend,' said Noddy, looking round. 'Big-Ears, where are you? Come with me on my very first drive in my very own car!'

Big-Ears got in – and off they went at top speed round and round the market place. 'Parp-parp! Parp-parp! Parp-parp!'

'It's the nicest car in the world,' said Noddy, delighted. 'And OH, Big-Ears! OH, I've got a WONDERFUL idea!'

'What?' asked Big-Ears.

'I'll be a taxi driver!' said Noddy, happily. 'I've got a car – I can take people wherever they want to go. Oh, Big-Ears – isn't that a fine idea? I've got my own job now – I'll drive my taxi.'

It is a good idea, little nodding man – and if ever we come to visit Toy Town, we'll ride in your taxi. Are you going to have any more adventures? Yes, of course you are. We'll read about them all another day!

LOOK OUT FOR NODDY'S
NEXT ADVENTURE

NODDY AND HIS CAR

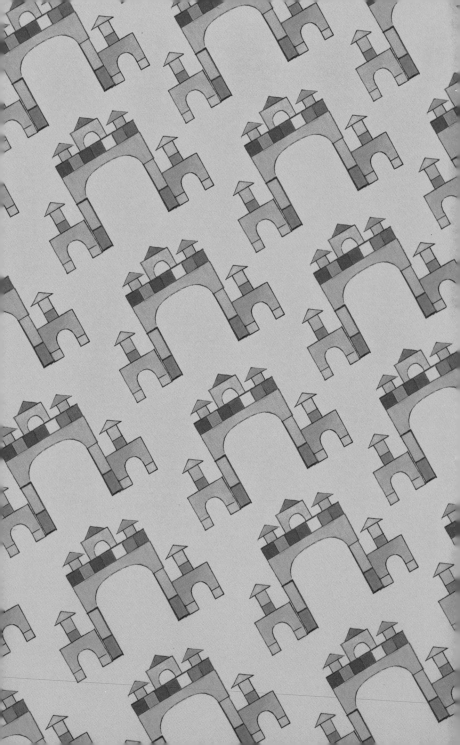